Breaking Point

Lesley Choyce

orca soundings

ORCA BOOK PUBLISHERS

Library and Archives Canada Cataloguing in Publication

Choyce, Lesley, 1951-
Breaking point / Lesley Choyce.
(Orca soundings)

Issued also in electronic formats.
ISBN 978-1-4598-0129-5 (bound).--ISBN 978-1-4598-0128-8 (pbk.)

I. Title. II. Series: Orca soundings
PS8555.H668B74 2012   JC813'.54   C2011-907836-8

First published in the United States, 2012
Library of Congress Control Number: 2011943734

Summary: Escaping from a wilderness camp for young offenders,
Cameron and Brianna end up in a struggle for survival.

*Orca Book Publishers is dedicated to preserving the environment and has printed
this book on paper certified by the Forest Stewardship Council®.*

Orca Book Publishers gratefully acknowledges the support for its publishing
programs provided by the following agencies: the Government of Canada
through the Canada Book Fund and the Canada Council for the Arts,
and the Province of British Columbia through the BC Arts Council
and the Book Publishing Tax Credit.

Cover photography ® Kablunk! / Masterfile

ORCA BOOK PUBLISHERS
PO Box 5626, Stn. B
Victoria, BC Canada
V8R 6S4

ORCA BOOK PUBLISHERS
PO Box 468
Custer, WA USA
98240-0468

www.orcabook.com
Printed and bound in Canada.

15 14 13 12 • 4 3 2 1

Chapter One

It was raining when I arrived at Camp Mosher on the Eastern Shore of Nova Scotia. Buckets of rain falling from a gray dead sky. I regretted my decision to come here. It was my choice. I could have been warm and dry up in the Valley in the so-called Nova Scotia Youth Facility in Walkerton. But I'd been there before and hated the dorks who were in charge.

So when they gave me the chance to go somewhere else, I jumped at it. Camp Mosher, just somewhere short of the end of the earth.

I got off the stupid bus, and as the other kids ran for the building, I just stood there in the rain and got soaked. I looked around. Nothing but trees, rocks and water. Lots of water. They had told me this would be different. That it would be tough. I'd have to learn about survival, about wilderness. About myself.

Don't get me wrong, I knew that was a pile of crap. And I'd never really had any interest in boats or camping or idiotic stuff like that. I just thought the deal was either three weeks here or ten weeks back in Walkerton. So here I was. I felt the rain soak all the way through my jacket and pants. I was cold and

I was drenched, and I could see I'd made a big fat mistake.

That's when some big asshole came up behind me, smacked me on the back and started pushing me toward the building. "They say turkeys are so stupid, they don't know when to get in out of the rain," he said as I tried to elbow him without turning around.

I thought about running just then. I didn't deserve to put up with this.

But I had nowhere to run to. Hell, I didn't really even know exactly where I was, except that I was on the coast of Nova Scotia, far from Halifax. Far from anywhere.

I turned around to look at the goon who was on my case. He was the size of a football player, and he had on some kind of rain poncho with the hood drooped down over his face. I guess my hands had automatically cramped up into fists, because the goon flipped his hood down and looked me in the eye. "Cameron, right?"

"Yeah," I said. He was big. Way out of my league.

"You like it out here?" he asked, an edge in his voice.

"Whaddaya mean?"

"You like the rain?"

"Yeah," I said. "Maybe I do."

I thought he was gonna shove me or drag me inside or something. But he didn't. "Okay for you, buddy," he said, flipping his poncho hood back up. "But this isn't the shopping mall. You're gonna have to stay dry if you want to survive."

And then he walked away.

I began to shiver. And that's when I looked to the inlet, saw the kayaks and canoes. There were even a few paddles. I thought all I'd have to do was run to the water, grab a boat and get the hell out of here.

Instead, I walked toward the main building, feeling like a loser, like I had nothing left of me.

Inside the building, I found myself in some kind of dining hall with shiny wood walls like you'd see in those old movies about kids going to summer camp. The windows were all steamed up. Some kids were walking around. Some were sitting. I recognized some of them as the losers who had come here on the bus with me from Halifax. But then I realized that there weren't just guys. There were girls here too. They must have arrived ahead of us on another bus. They were all sitting at tables on the other side of the room.

I just stood there dripping water on the floor. I didn't know which I hated more—standing out in the rain, or standing here inside the door with all those eyes looking at me like I was the biggest loser in the place. Again, I was ready to just turn and run. That was my style. I was a runner. When I found myself freaking out in school, or when the shit hit the fan, or when I'd do some idiot thing that was about to get me in big trouble, I'd spin on my heels and run. That's the way I'd saved my ass a dozen times, caught inside people's houses when I was ripping them off.

I always got away.

Well, not always.

But here, now, with everyone staring at me, where the hell was I going to run to?

That's when I saw her. She was staring at me. But not like the others. They all had some kind of smirk or goofy smile. She looked like she felt sorry for me. Her eyes were fixed on me, and when I made eye contact, I couldn't look away. Her long dark hair was wet, and it was clinging to the sides of her face, framing it. And the way she was looking at me made me feel like she knew who I was. *Really* knew me. Who was this girl?

That's when the big guy walked over to me. "If you want some dry clothes, follow me."

I didn't know what else to do. I couldn't stand there all day. I wanted to talk to that girl, but that wasn't going to work in front of all the others. So I followed the dude.

"I'm Chris," he said as he led me out of the dining hall and down a hallway. "You'll be seeing a lot of me. I'm not exactly going to be your best friend. But I'm not a total pain in the ass either."

He pointed to a storage room, and I saw the clothes hanging up on racks. I walked in. Chris didn't follow. "Just come back and join us when you've found some stuff that fits."

I found a hoodie and some pants and somebody's old running shoes that fit. I cursed myself again for ending up here. For getting caught. For getting that lousy judge who decided to make things hard on me instead of just giving me the usual slap on the wrist. Everything sucked big-time. I wanted to scream.

So I did.

A few seconds later, Chris poked his head back in the room, although he didn't seem particularly concerned. "Guess this isn't the happiest day of your life?"

"I've had worse," I said.

"I've been where you are. I know it feels like shit."

"And this is supposed to cheer me up?"

"Not at all. Just wanted you to know. Come have something to eat. Food used to be crap here. But it's improved."

So I followed him back to the hall, but when I got there, the girls were all gone. She wasn't there. Chris led me to the food counter and handed me a tray. When I got my food and sat down at the closest table, two guys at the table started laughing. I wanted to scream for a second time.

But I didn't. I pretended they weren't there. I decided to think about something, anything that would keep me from losing it. So I pictured her face. Her eyes. I wondered how I was going to get to meet this girl.

Chapter Two

I kept to myself that first day and tried to keep my head down. The rain pounded on the metal roof through the night, and then it suddenly stopped at around 3:00 AM. I was lying there on my bunk thinking that I didn't deserve this. I'd screwed up and got caught. I'd spent time at Walkerton before, where I'd learned more tricks of the trade from other kids there. Then I'd gone back home and used what I'd learned. Breaking and entering. It's a skill like any other one. Even with security systems, it was usually a piece of cake. What I hadn't factored in was unmarked, silent video surveillance.

In the morning the sun was out. By 8:30, twelve of us were standing on the shoreline of the inlet wearing life jackets or PFDS—personal flotation devices. In front of each of us was a sea kayak. Chris handed me a two-bladed paddle and pointed to the red kayak in front of me. I looked at it and then out at the water. I have to admit, I liked what I saw—blue, sparkling and beautiful.

Chris gave this big boring lecture about safety, and I didn't pay much attention. I kept thinking about the girl. And then we were finally on the water.

I was snug inside the kayak with the spray skirt, the piece of rubber meant to keep water out, tight around my waist. It was like the kayak was part of me. At first it felt pretty wobbly, but as I got moving, things smoothed out and I was thinking, Hey, this is easy. I'm loving this.

We were all together in a group, headed toward a rocky island ahead. I felt like I needed some more space, so I took a deep stroke with my paddle and split off to the left. The sun in my face and the smell of salt water all around made me a little dizzy, and I was thinking I hadn't felt this good in a long, long time. But then I heard someone yelling. Chris.

"Cameron. Get back with us. Don't screw around."

Well, I guess I knew that was coming. Only thing is, I had this little voice in my head that said, *Don't do it. Just keep going.*

So I did.

"Cameron. Back here now!" I heard Chris scream.

I could have been a good boy and done what I was told. But that wasn't my style. I just kept paddling, straight into the morning sun. Straight off into oblivion on my own. It wasn't like I was trying to split. I just wanted to go where I wanted to go.

I was always listening to that voice in my head. It said things like, *You can do it. You'll get away with it. You'll never be caught.*

By then, I knew that Chris had struck out of the pack and was headed after me. That was inevitable. He wasn't going to let me just paddle off into the wilderness. Then I made the mistake of turning around to see how close he was.

I guess I leaned too far to the left and then lost my balance. *Wham.* I went over.

I can't begin to describe the shock to my system. The water was icy cold. I was completely upside down with my kayak above me. I flailed the paddle underwater, but that didn't seem to do any good, so I let go of it.

I wanted to scratch my way up to the surface so badly. But the worst part was I couldn't get out of the kayak. I was still sealed into place by the spray skirt. And I was upside down. I hadn't paid attention to the part of the lecture about how to rip the skirt off the kayak, how to push downward, out of a kayak when you are upside down.

I thrashed about and felt my lungs begin to burn. My brain was screaming at me to get to the surface, but no matter how hard I twisted and turned, I couldn't get free to swim up. I was totally panicked.

And then suddenly I saw the shadow of something above me on the water's surface. I saw an arm push down into the water, and then a hand grabbed my wrist and yanked hard.

I twisted free of the kayak and felt myself being pulled upward. I surfaced a second later, gasping for air and snorting seawater out my nose. When I could catch my breath, I saw Chris scowling at me, but he didn't say a word.

I draped myself across the front of his kayak to get some breath and my bearings. I wondered what would happen next.

"You got the balls to get back into your own kayak, or you want me to just haul your sorry ass back to shore?" he asked.

I was cold and still pretty freaked by what had just happened. "I don't know, man," I said.

He looked at me for second. "If you can follow directions, we can do this."

I looked around me and realized how far from shore we were. Once again, I had been the screwup. I decided I would let Chris call the shots. I nodded at him.

"Okay, you've got your life jacket on, so you're not gonna drown. So slip off my boat and get back in the water."

I looked at him like he was crazy.

"Just do it."

I eased back into the icy-cold seawater.

"Now lift the nose of your kayak onto mine."

My kayak was still upside down and seemed to weigh a ton. I struggled with it as Chris braced his kayak with his paddle to stay steady. Eventually, I got the front tip of my kayak on top of his and he reached forward with one arm to slide it up and over. I realized then just how strong this guy was.

When most of the water had emptied, Chris flipped it upright and back down in the water like it was nothing at all. I was still dog-paddling and cold as hell. He braced my boat and then said, "Get in. Nice and easy."

I floundered and slipped and struggled but eventually got back in. He handed me my paddle. There was still water in the bottom of my boat, but at least I was back in it.

"You want me to take you back to camp, or you want to catch up with the others and go to that island out there?" He pointed to the rocky island we had originally been heading for. "I got a pack of dry clothes here you can change into. It's not the first time, you know."

I nodded to the island and took a stroke with my paddle. My heart was still racing pretty fast.

"Great," he said. "Just don't be an asshole again."

Chapter Three

When we got to the island, I was still wet and shaking from the cold. I got some razzing from the other guys, but I'd taken much worse in my time. I walked off with the packet of dry clothes to change and found myself standing on a large rock shelf in the morning sun overlooking the inlet.

I skinned off my wet clothes and stood naked for a couple of minutes, letting the sun dry me. In front of me was the bright blue water, and out there were dozens of islands in the distance as far as I could see. I knew I was looking east. I'd seen the map of this place. I knew that in this direction there were no roads and no towns for a long, long way. Nothing but sea and islands. It would not be hard to get lost out there.

I put on the clothes, which were a little too big for me, and walked back to join the others. Chris didn't say anything else about what I'd done. I watched as he lit a fire, and half listened as he gave a talk about wilderness survival. That word, *survival*, echoed in my head. I'd just had my own close call. That's what I was struggling for down there underwater. Survival. The basic instinct to live.

But wasn't that what it was all about? Even back in civilization. We were all just trying to get by. We all just wanted to survive by getting what we needed to live. But why was it so difficult?

I was a nervous paddler on the way back to the camp later that morning. I trailed behind the others, but everyone left me alone, even Chris. When I allowed myself to stop beating myself up, I looked around again and thought that being on the water like this was great. But, as always, something was gnawing at me. I felt like an animal in a cage, even out here in the wide-open watery inlet. No matter what I did in life, I couldn't shake it.

Back in the hall at lunchtime, I sat by myself at the end of a table in the back of the room. I'd always been a loner, so this was nothing new. Back home at school, they had names for me. I never had many friends, and those I did have were ones who'd get me in trouble. Most times, I thought I was better off on my own.

I spotted her in the lunch line and wondered what her morning had been like. I didn't think she had seen me when she walked in, but as soon as she left the line with her tray of food, it was like the girl had some kind of radar, because she walked straight in my direction and sat down across from me.

"I hear you nearly drowned," she said.

"News travels fast."

"Around here it does. Anyway, no big deal. I'm not afraid of death. Are you?"

"A little," I said.

"You'll get over it."

It was an odd conversation with someone I had never spoken to before, but she was interesting, for sure. Different. And she was hot.

"I'm Brianna," she said.

"Cameron."

"Do people call you Cam?"

"No."

"Ouch. Okay, Cameron. You okay with me sitting here, or you want me to leave?"

"Sorry," I said. I knew I had just sent out a bad vibe, and I sure as hell didn't want her to leave.

"It's okay. You had a rough morning, nearly drowning and all."

"What did you do?" I asked. My social skills were not all that polished.

"What do you mean?"

"What did you do that landed you here?"

"Oh, that. You really want to know?"

"Yeah."

"I got busted for selling weed at school."

"At school, really?"

"Well, weed and a little E. But the E wasn't really my thing. It was just the once."

"And you got caught."

"Yeah. Again. I'm what they refer to as incorrigible. A repeat offender."

"I've been labeled that before."

"Maybe we can form a club," she said. "Or a band. The Incorrigibles."

"Maybe. You been to Walkerton?"

"Twice."

"And now you're here. Like me."

"That's us. But you didn't tell me what you did."

"Broke into people's houses and stole things."

"That wasn't nice," she said, a half smile sneaking out, making me realize just how pretty this drug-dealing incorrigible girl was.

"I can't even tell you why I did it. I just tried it once and it was easy, so I did it some more. Kept some things. Sold some stuff for some pocket money."

"It was probably the thrill," she said. "You liked the buzz of the danger and you liked breaking rules."

"Is that why you sold drugs?"

"Not drugs. Like I said, mostly weed. But no, I was in it for the money. I still plan on making a million dollars before I turn twenty-one."

"Still?"

"Well, yeah. Once I get out of this shithole and make my way out of Nova Scotia. I have connections. What about you? Future plans?"

I threw up my hands. "I'm more of a one-day-at-a-time kind of guy."

She looked a little disappointed. "We could work on that," she said. "You like me?"

That one threw me, but then everything about this girl threw me. I cleared my throat so that I had a chance to think before speaking. I wanted it to sound just right. "Yeah," I said. "I'm just getting to know you, but I like what I see."

"And what is it you see?" she shot back.

"I see fire," I said. I didn't even know where that came from, but it lit her up. She liked it. What I was thinking was, I see a drug-dealing girl who is very attractive and nothing but trouble, looking for trouble and looking to get *me* in more trouble. But I didn't say that.

Chapter Four

It rained for five days after that. Most of what we did was inside. Exercise classes, talking sessions with the counselors—real wannabe social workers. They were all pretty young and clueless. They said things like, "You have your whole life ahead of you. You can control your life. You are in charge."

If I was in charge, I would have been out of there. In fact, the pressure was building up inside me. When the weather got better, I could do that. I could run. Into the woods. Anywhere. I didn't really want to go back home. I didn't know where I wanted to go. But yeah, maybe it was time for me to take charge.

They kept the guys separated from the girls during that week. There must have been problems, because now they kept us apart even at meals. I could wave to Brianna and she'd look at me, but we couldn't actually talk. I kept thinking about that girl.

A guy in the room where I slept, Gerard, kept on my case like he wanted to fight. Why me? I wondered. Just because I had *Loser* stamped in big red letters on my forehead, I guessed. Growing up, I'd known at least twenty Gerards. They zero in on you for no particular reason. They piss you off. They know they can beat the crap out of you. All you have to do is let your guard down or, worse yet, fake being tough.

Gerard was cold one night and ripped the blanket off my bed for himself. He didn't say a word. I waited until he fell asleep, and then I took it back. I did it gently so he didn't wake up. My style. There was a night-light in the room, so a few of the guys who were awake saw me. Then I turned around, put my butt up close to his sleeping face and farted. Fortunately for me, he didn't wake, but I'd made my point.

Someone must have reported my nighttime activities, because in the morning Gerard snarled at me and called me a name or two that had a familiar ring. I pretended I didn't hear him. Gerard threatened to get me good when I wasn't looking, and I knew he wasn't kidding. More reason to get the hell out of here.

But I didn't turn him in. I could have told Chris, but then I would have to be watching my own back all the time. There were some rules you just had to play by.

Finally the skies cleared and we were outside again. I found myself on a team of guys playing volleyball against a team of girls. Freaking volleyball. I hadn't played that since I was a little kid in junior high. But playing against the girls was definitely all right. I guess they thought we were safe if they kept the net between us. And there was Brianna on the other team. When it was my turn to serve, I hit the ball straight to her and she made a nice return right in my direction. I flubbed my own return, but I still felt like we had connected. Hey, I guess, under the circumstances, it was about as romantic as things could get.

And then a few days later, we were back in the kayaks and on a longer trip. No splashdowns for me. No wipe-outs. This trip out was an overnighter to an island. Each of us had a tiny little tent. Privacy at last. The day had been sunny, and I had a burnt nose. But my paddling was good, the exercise had me tired, and I slept like a baby in my own tiny private tent.

It must have been after midnight when I heard the zipper to my tent. Oh shit, I thought. It's either a frigging bear come to eat me, or it's Gerard. I groped for my flashlight, hoping it was the bear. If I was going out of this world, I'd rather be a meal for a wild animal than the victim of a bully-creep like Gerard.

I finally found my little flashlight and flicked it on straight at my intruder.

Boy, had I called that one wrong.

Kneeling at the opening of my tent was Brianna. Her eyes were wide, and she pulled herself quickly in. "Shh," was all she said. "Turn off your light."

I was propped up on my elbows trying to get her into focus and figure out what was going on. She was the one to reach out and turn the flashlight off. The tent went pitch-black. Then she lay down beside me. I could hear her breathing heavily.

"Where'd you come from?" I asked.

"You didn't know? Some of us are camping on the other end of the island. It's not that big. I planned this."

I was thinking, Planned? This was part of some plan? But was I ever happy to see her. Well, I couldn't see her. But I was happy she was here. How could I not be? She leaned back and zipped my tent up again. "Mosquitoes out there. Very nasty."

"How'd you get here?"

"Walked the shoreline. I'd studied the map before we left. I heard the news that you guys would be here. I wanted to find you. I saw your pack outside." She lay down beside me on her back and grew quiet. I lay beside her and listened to her breathe. Now what? I wondered.

I had the distinct feeling that whatever would come out of my mouth would be wrong, and I didn't want to screw things up, so I said nothing. I wanted to reach over and hold her. It had been so long since I'd had my arms around a girl. But I couldn't take the chance. I wanted to turn on my flashlight and maybe even just look at her. But I didn't do that either.

"Ever feel like every single important decision you've made in your life is wrong?" she suddenly asked.

"I know the feeling," I said.

"Let's make it change."

"How?"

"Come with me to Montreal?"

"Montreal?" Was she crazy? We were in a remote camp for young criminals on the Eastern Shore of Nova Scotia. Montreal was a long way away.

"I know some people there. We get there, and we can disappear. A couple of fake driver's licenses and a new life. I can't do it alone. I picked you."

I wanted to say, *Why me?* But I'd seen that look she gave me the first day. Yes, it was like we connected. Something electric. Fire.

Chapter Five

She leaned over me and brushed my cheek lightly with her hand. Then she kissed me on the mouth. I put my arms around her. I was starting to think this might be one hell of a night, but she pulled back.

"Plenty of time for that," she said. "But I can't stay here. I can't get caught. I just need to know you'll do this with me."

Yikes. I didn't even know this girl, but I was ready to follow her to the ends of the earth. I asked the obvious question. "Do what?"

"I'm good with maps. I know where we are. I know what's around us. East of here, there's not much but wilderness, empty shorelines and islands for almost thirty miles. If we can make it through those islands without being seen, I've got a cousin in Port Joseph. My aunt and uncle moved there from the city when she started to get into trouble. We've stayed in touch. We know the same people in Montreal. She has a car. If we could get to Port Joseph, she'd drive us. We wouldn't have to put up with any more of this crap."

"You make it sound easy. It would be a long hike. You sure we could find this Port Joseph place?"

"Yeah, we'll find it, but we're not going to walk. We go by water. With all those islands, we'd be much harder to find."

I was remembering my first dip in the icy waters around here. Chris had said that we'd been taking easy routes, protected from the wind and the waves and the difficulties of paddling long distances on open water. "Sounds dangerous," I said, probably sounding like a wimp.

"Not if we're smart."

"And lucky."

"Yeah, that too," she said. "But I feel it in my bones. This is what I need to do. Walk away from my old crappy life. This is the decision that will finally change my life." She leaned over and kissed me again. "And I need you."

Once again, I wanted to blurt out, *Why me?*

But I didn't.

"I'm in," I said.

She put a hand on each side of my face and gently squeezed like I was a puppy or a little kid. She laughed a little. "I knew you would be. Cameron. You won't regret it, I promise." And I liked the sound of that so much that I was a little stunned.

And then she was up and unzipping the tent door, slipping out into the night and gone.

A mosquito flew in through the open flap and bit me on the ear. I swatted it and smacked myself hard on the side of the head. Then I reached over and zipped the flap.

I should have smacked myself harder. Maybe I would have smacked some sense into myself. Maybe I would have used my brain to make a decision for once instead of my emotions. Maybe everything would have turned out differently.

But my head was swimming with Brianna. This crazy, beautiful, dangerous drug-dealing girl who had just been in my tent. I couldn't fall back asleep, so I tried to picture us on the road to Montreal, arriving there and starting a new life. The two of us together. The whole scene was very sweet.

But the more I got caught up in this fantasy, the more I began to think that I didn't know what I was getting into. Leaping from the frying pan into the fire? Yeah, she *was* fire. And what if I got burned? And yet, I knew that if I changed my mind and turned her down, she'd choose someone else. Maybe even Gerard.

And I couldn't let that happen. Not in a million years.

I didn't see her again the next day, as our group kayaked out around a bunch of small windswept islands. There were seabirds all around and seals in the water and lounging on rocks. An eagle sailed above me once. And lots and lots of open water.

They had planned it so we would never run into the girls, who must have gone in another direction. But I could see what Brianna was talking about. This was a wild, empty and uninhabited part of Nova Scotia. If we could get away, there would be a million tiny coves to hide in, hundreds of islands where we could go ashore and hole up. If you wanted to hide, it would take an entire navy to find you in this vast expanse of water and islands.

Even traveling with my fellow criminals and following Chris's directions, out here I felt free and alive and in control of my own kayak and, somehow, my own fate. I only knew the basics of Brianna's escape plan, but the more

I thought about it, the more I began to believe Brianna and I had the stuff to make it happen.

I'd be alone with her out here—daytime and at night. And that would be a dream come true. Who cares if we never made it to Montreal? And it wasn't like we were breaking out of Walkerton. This was different—bigger and more exciting than that. And this would prove that we were more powerful than the rotten, unfair system that put us here. The one that was always trying to break us.

My arms were starting to get a bit sore and my back was feeling it when Chris veered away from leading the group and doubled back, and then came up alongside me. "Cameron, you're a strong paddler. You're a natural at this. How do you feel?"

"I feel great."

"I watched you this morning. You seemed different."

That worried me. Did he suspect something?

"I meant that in a good way."

"Oh. Thanks."

"We have a group of younger kids coming in for a day camp next week. I'm wondering if you'd help me teach them some of the basics about water safety and handling kayaks."

That was a weird request. Me? A role model for young delinquents? But hey, why not? It would give me brownie points.

But then, maybe Brianna and I would be long gone by the time the young hoodlums arrived. Nonetheless, I wanted Chris to think I was dependable. "Sure," I said. "I'd love to."

Chapter Six

Back at the camp, it was business as usual. Gerard giving me crap. Chris trying to be my friend and mentor. Me with one voice in my head telling me to chill and see this camp thing through, go back to school in the fall. Be good. And the other voice saying, *Go for the girl. Run. Get the hell out of here. Go crazy. Start a new exciting life.*

But then things got a little complicated.

It started as a food fight in the dining hall. The girls. I was watching Brianna from across the room. I'm pretty sure she started it. Somebody accidentally shoved against her as she was eating.

Brianna shoved back—hard. And then the other girl, a tall big-shouldered one with short cropped hair, said something nasty. That's when Brianna took her fork and flicked something— mashed potatoes I think—into her face. That was all it took.

The big girl dropped her tray to the floor and reached for Brianna's hair, grabbed it and pulled her backward. Brianna reached behind her for the girl's head and smacked her in the ears.

Then all hell broke loose.

The two girls were fighting, and everyone was up and yelling. I felt sick to my stomach and tried to push my way through the crowd to help Brianna, but I couldn't get there.

Chris and a couple of the women counselors were pulling people apart and trying to get to the fighting girls, and when they did, Chris held his hands up to the mob to get some control while the two women pulled the girls apart. Brianna was pulled off, still swinging her arms and looking fierce. She didn't look hurt, but the other girl had a bloody nose.

I tried to make eye contact with her, and I yelled her name, but she was still struggling to free herself. Her arms were pinned behind her back by the woman counselor, and when I saw the handcuffs snapped on her wrists, I realized that these were not just youth counselors. These were trained corrections workers. I yelled Brianna's name again, but she wasn't looking my way.

Both girls were led out of the dining hall, and soon after, so was everyone else.

We were confined to our rooms for the night. When Chris came in, I asked him about Brianna.

"She's in isolation," he said. "So is the other girl. Five days. That's the rule."

"Just like Walkerton," I said.

"Not exactly. But we have to impose discipline." Chris studied me. "You like this girl, right?"

I thought it was better not to say too much. After all, we had plans, Brianna and I. Plans to get the hell out of here.

"No," I said. "Just curious. I was starting to think of this as more like summer camp than prison."

"Think of it as summer camp with a few serious rules."

"Right."

That night, I thought of my own time in isolation at Walkerton. My first time, I had no idea how hard it was to be truly, truly alone, locked in a room with nothing but the stupid crazy thoughts going through your head. I hated every minute of it. I screamed out loud sometimes. I banged on the door. I got really antsy and thought I was losing my mind. And then I even cried. Cried like a baby. Isolation was tough. It was mean what it did to you. It's not exactly like torture. You have no control. You have nothing. Nothing but yourself.

And in my case, I'm not always that fond of my own company.

I could imagine what this was doing to Brianna.

So I played it cool. Went to bed, waited for everyone to be asleep, and then I got up and put my clothes on.

I really didn't know how they worked security here. Sometimes it seemed pretty slack. Other times you could see they could be serious. We all had been chosen to come here because it was believed we wouldn't run. None of us wanted to get shipped to Walkerton, and we knew if we screwed up, we'd be there in a flash and we'd have a longer stay.

But I really needed to find Brianna and see if she was okay. I scrambled low across the floor and out into the dimly lit hallway. One of the women counselors seemed to be on duty at a desk near the front door—the only way out of here. But she was watching a little portable TV and I think she had earphones in her ears. I guessed that Brianna was still somewhere in the building. I turned and headed to the farthest end of the hall.

At the last doorway, I stopped, crouched low and listened. Nothing. I tried the handle. Locked, of course. "Brianna," I whispered. Nothing. Then a little louder.

"Cameron?" I heard her voice coming from a door across the hall.

I slid across the floor and put my ear close to it. "You okay?" I asked.

"I hate this. I can't handle being alone. Get me out."

I knew that if I did, I'd get caught. There was no way I could break open the door. Then we'd both be in isolation. "I can't."

"But I need you," she said. I heard the panic in her voice.

"You'll get through this," I said. "Think about something else. Think about us. Think about your plan. We'll do it." I said this with conviction, even though I was having more than second thoughts. After seeing Brianna in a fight, I knew that this could be one mean, tough girl. Was that really the person I wanted to hitch myself to?

"We have to get out of here. Now," she said.

If I knew one thing, I knew that now was not the time. "No. You have to ride this out. We have to be on our best behavior. Then no one will suspect anything. I'll come visit you at night like this. Then, when you get out, we can't be seen together too much. We don't want them to see us like that."

There was silence at first, and then she said something that was like a bombshell. "But I love you," she said. There was desperation in her voice.

"And I love you too," I heard myself say. But the words scared the crap out of me.

Chapter Seven

I don't know how I did it, but I watched and waited each night for a quiet time to go sit in the hallway and talk to Brianna. I could never stay long, but I knew she really needed it. Funny thing about girls. I'd never really had a girlfriend. Some girls liked me, but those girls I found boring. The girls I liked tended to be bad girls—troublemakers

at school, girls who got into some bad
stuff out in the world. But none of them
ever seemed interested in me.

Now, I guess I'd found a girl—Brianna.
I had finally found my very own bad girl.

Three days into Brianna's isolation,
the younger kids arrived for a day visit.
Some of my fellow inmates were sent
off on kayak trips, but about twenty of
us were left behind to act as "guides"
for the visiting rug rats. Chris explained
that it was a new idea. An experiment.
"But you have to do it right. Talk to
your guest and get to know him. Tell
him about the camp, about you. It's your
chance to be a role model."

"I've never been a role model for
anything." The whole idea seemed
ridiculous.

"Give it a shot. You do well, and it
will look good on you."

I knew that this was some kind of
test. Chris was giving me responsibility

and "believing in me." It wasn't like I was going to teach the kid to break into people's houses. I could play the game.

The kid's name was Philip. He was twelve, and he arrived on a bus from the city with the others. Chris introduced me to him and told us the ground rules. Everyone had to stay between the camp building and the water, and we could play games, talk, do silly art projects or just hang out. Chris handed a set of questions to me and a set to Philip. We were supposed to ask each other these things to get to know each other. It seemed totally lame, but I knew if I played it well, this day would set me up to look really trustworthy.

And that would make it easier to escape with Brianna when the time came.

Philip was about the most unhappy little kid I'd ever seen. I hadn't spent much time around younger kids and found it hard at first to even get him talking. We both went through our list of questions giving one- or two-word answers and rolling our eyes about the whole thing. Chris and the other workers hung back at a distance, but they were watching us, so I played along with things.

Philip and I were sitting on a wooden picnic table a bit off from the others. When the questions were over, he just sat there looking off at the water. His face said it all. He was hurt and he was angry, and for a minute I was speechless. Then I realized what I was feeling. I was feeling sorry for this poor little slob. Philip was a bigger walking disaster than I was.

I cleared my throat. "You ever want any lessons in all the wrong things to do in life, just ask me. I'm the king of bad decisions."

He blinked but didn't turn to look at me. He stared out at the water like he wasn't even there.

"So give me something to work with here. I need to look like I'm good at this…whatever *this* is."

He turned then and looked straight at me. "What the hell do you want me to do?" Philip snapped. "I hate this shit. I hate being here. And I hate my life. Work with that, asshole."

It caught me off guard. The little snot had quite the mouth on him. At first I was pissed. Who the hell was he to talk to me like that? But instead of giving the kid my own real thoughts about him or this whole charade, I laughed. "Why don't you tell me what you really feel?" I asked sarcastically.

That got just the slightest hint of a smile.

"You do know I'm here because I broke a couple of laws, right?" I asked.

"Yeah. Duh. And you think I'm here as a reward for being good?"

"Dunno. What'd you do?"

"Accidentally stabbed a kid at school?"

"Accidentally?"

"It was his knife. He was coming at me."

"But you took the rap?" I asked.

"I took the knife. And we were fighting. Shit happens. It wasn't like I was trying to kill him or anything."

"Is that why you're so unhappy?"

"No. I'm used to getting blamed for things that aren't my fault."

"Then what is it?"

He looked straight at me again, now seeming older. Much older. "Hey, Cameron, or whatever your freaking name is, let's pretend we like each other so we can get through this. So I can go home at the end of the day, and you can look like you did your good deed for the day and go back to your bunk bed. But don't try to be my big brother."

Then he looked away.

"Deal," I said.

"Great." And he smiled the fakest smile I'd ever seen.

Things didn't improve much after that, but we did get through the day. I showed him the kayaks and let him sit in one on dry land. We had lunch together, and I showed him my room. We made some small talk, but he never lost the attitude. I got really pissed off at him a few times but held back from saying anything nasty.

And when he got back on the bus, he didn't bother to say goodbye.

When he was gone, Chris came over to me. "How'd it go?"

"Great. He's got a few issues, but deep down I think he's a good kid."

"He was the toughest one of the lot. I assigned him to you. You know why?"

"Why?"

"'Cause he reminded me of you," Chris said. "All that hurt. And attitude."

"I think maybe we bonded," I lied to him, reminding myself this was all about appearances and looking like I was dependable.

"You're not a very good liar," he said. "But I give you credit for making it through the day without smacking him. That's a step in the right direction." And Chris walked off, leaving me sitting there thinking about Philip, feeling truly sorry for him and wishing I had done a better job of making friends with the kid. And then suddenly I realized I wasn't feeling sorry for him. I was feeling sorry for me.

Chapter Eight

So after my shining performance as a mentor for a young hoodlum, I was thinking I could get away with just about anything. I'd been able to sneak down the hall and talk to Brianna for four nights in a row. But on her last night in isolation, things were different.

Chris was bunking in the hall. He said it was because the screen was out in his room and there were too many mosquitoes, and he said he couldn't sleep with the window closed. But maybe he'd heard rumors about me and Brianna.

I was pretty worried, because Brianna had been getting more and more edgy. In fact, I was scared that she would make a run for it as soon as she was let out of isolation. To be honest, the girl was getting crazier. But she had me hooked. I didn't want to lose her. And I had a feeling that if she ran on her own, she would be in big trouble. I'm not trying to say I'm some knight in shining armor or anything. I'm nobody's hero, but I think she needed me.

When I saw her the morning of her release, she looked frantic. I knew that she'd been in a comfortable room and she'd had food and she'd been safe. This whole summer camp for bad kids was a piece of cake compared to the real institutions. But isolation is still isolation. And she was probably pissed at me for not showing up last night as promised.

I caught her eye at breakfast, but she looked away. Damn. I knew I couldn't walk over to her right then. Not here and not now. Gerard saw me looking. "She's hot," he said. "Looks like she's lost interest in you. Maybe it's my turn."

I gave Gerard a look that could have burned him to the ground, but I didn't say anything. If I did something stupid, I'd end up in isolation for five days. And then what? I looked back at Brianna and silently mouthed the word, "Sorry." I think she understood, but she quickly looked away again.

Later that morning, we were all outside getting lectured by Chris (who seemed to always know everything about everything) on wilderness survival. I wasn't really paying attention. I heard the part about how rough kayaking can get if the waves come up or if there is strong wind. Then he mentioned that we probably wouldn't be in the water for the next week. A tropical storm, possibly a hurricane, was headed straight for Nova Scotia. Kids sounded pretty disappointed.

Then he said we'd take a break, and I cautiously walked over to where Brianna sat.

"Why didn't you come talk to me last night?" she asked. She looked both hurt and angry.

"I couldn't."

"Why not?"

I explained about Chris sleeping in the hall.

"I was scared. I needed you. I hated being alone. I can never, ever do that again."

I knew where this was headed. "I know," I said. "You all right?"

"We need to talk," she said.

"Here?"

"Somewhere."

"Let me say something to Chris. I'll tell him you aren't feeling well and I'm just going to walk you in to sit down in the dining hall. I think he'll let me." I explained about Philip and my fake mentor role. Mr. Responsible. Mr. Dependable. Mr. Role Model.

Chris was totally cool about it. I knew I had just moved to another level with him. I knew he thought this camp thing was working—at least for me. But he didn't have a clue.

Inside, we sat by ourselves at a table. There were two counselors in with the kitchen staff. They could see us, but they left us alone.

"I'm leaving tonight," she said. I knew that was coming.

"Then I'm coming with you. Montreal, right?"

"Yeah. All we have to do is get to my cousin and she'll drive us."

I felt a chill go down my spine. I didn't want to do this. But if I didn't, I'd lose her.

"I don't think going by kayak is a good idea," I said.

"It's the only way. They'd find us if we went by road, and I don't think I could find my way through the woods. All we have to do is go east. I figure two or three days of straight paddling and we'll be at Port Joseph."

"How are we going to be sure which way is east?" I asked.

"There's a compass built into some of the kayaks."

"Is that like a GPS?"

"It's the old way. I know how to use one."

"But didn't you hear Chris? There's a tropical storm headed this way. Big winds, big waves."

"Look outside. It's beautiful. I say it's tonight or never."

Her mind was made up. I wanted to tell her she was crazy. I wanted to say we'll never make it. I wanted to say we should just be patient, be good, make it through the rest of our time here, and then we'd be back in the city. But I knew if we did that, she would split and I'd never see her again. Besides, I knew she wouldn't stay here. She was like a trapped animal.

I also knew that if Chris or any of them were sleeping in the hallway, we'd never get out without being seen.

"Are you in or out?" It was an ultimatum. She was looking straight at me. Her face was close to mine. Although her tone was tough, her look was soft. She was beautiful.

"I love you," I said. And I think she got the point.

Chapter Nine

I didn't speak to her again all that day. We agreed to that. And we agreed to meet at the kayak shed down by the water at eleven o'clock at night. I had a bad feeling in my gut. I didn't want to admit I was scared. I didn't trust kayaks or the inlet or a million things that could go wrong out there. But what else could I do?

I lay in my bunk breathing raggedly, loud enough for Gerard to ask me to shut up. At ten minutes to eleven by my watch, I got up to pretend I was going to take a leak. The hallway was clear. Someone had fixed the screen in Chris's room, I reckoned. There was no sign of Brianna, but I knew she'd be there. Or at least, I knew she would leave.

I crept low along the hall. One of the other counselors had his room right by the entrance. His door was open, but a TV was on inside and maybe he was asleep. Who knows? All I knew was that the door to the outside was unlocked. Had Brianna already left? It swung open without a sound, and I closed it just as silently.

Outside, it was very dark. I realized we should be waiting for first light in the morning. Leaving in the dark was insane. Everything about this was insane.

We had no maps. No supplies. I had the jacket on my back, that's all.

I ran for the boathouse and slipped inside, where it was even darker than outside. I waited for my eyes to adjust. Then I saw her. She had found a pack and was shoving things into it.

"Brianna."

"The weather's good," she said. "No wind. No waves. I've got a few things that were around here. I have a good feeling about this."

"Me too," I lied. My eyes were a little adjusted now. I needed to get my wits about me and make sure we did this right. I reached for the life jackets and tossed her one.

She tossed it back. "I don't think we need these things. You can swim, right?"

Well, the answer would have been, "barely." But it wasn't about swimming. It was about surviving in that cold

North Atlantic water if we dumped. "Brianna, you have to wear one." My tone was harsh, insistent.

There was a pause, and I caught a glimpse of her face. I thought she was about to tell me to get lost. Instead she said, rather sarcastically, "Fine." And she put on the life jacket and snapped the clasps. I did the same. I knew we were carving out new territory here. I'd been reckless all my life, and now I'd hitched myself to someone more reckless than me. Great.

"This one," she said, lifting a red kayak from the rack. "Grab that end. Walk it to the water." I took the orders this time. Then we went back for a second one that was orange. Lift, haul. We went back for the pack, paddles and spray skirts.

On the shore of the inlet, not a breath of air was moving. You could hear bugs, and tiny waves lapping, and there was now a quarter moon giving us a little light. We got into the kayaks in shallow water, and I waited as she pushed off.

I almost didn't go. I almost chickened out.

But suddenly she was out there, a dark silhouette in a long narrow boat, already moving away quickly on the dark but sparkling water. And my heart sank. I had no choice. I pushed off the shallow bottom with my paddle, heard the hull of the kayak scraping over sand and pebbles, and then I was free of land.

I wobbled a few times but paddled harder until my speed made me more stable. It took some serious effort to catch up with her. She was a strong paddler. When I came up alongside her boat, I could see the determination in her face.

"We did it," she said, smiling. "We're free. I'm never, ever gonna let anyone put me through that again."

"How do you know we're headed the right way?"

"The compass, remember?" she said, pointing to where it sat mounted on the front deck of her kayak. "Trust me. Besides, I know the first part of this. Remember the night I came to you in your tent? We're headed there first. But we shouldn't stay there. We might be found. There's an island just past that called Ram Island, and we can tuck into a tiny cove. Then leave early in the morning."

We heard things moving in the waters around us. Seals, I was hoping. But I didn't know. I had grown up in a city. What did I know about creatures out in the sea at night? All I could do was paddle my brains out to keep up with Brianna. The quarter moon was just barely large enough so that we could see. If anything went wrong... well, I just didn't even want to go there. All I knew was that there was no turning back.

It must have been well after midnight when we rounded the island where we had camped. In another twenty minutes we came in close to Ram Island on the landward side, and the world went wonderfully silent. I suddenly felt totally ecstatic. We were making it. There was the cove, just as she had said, and some sand. We slid our kayaks up onto the pocket beach. I jumped out first and pulled her boat farther up on shore.

I stood there in the moonlight, breathing hard from all the exercise and feeling more than a little high. Stunned would be a better word. We were both looking back at the water from where we came when Brianna suddenly turned around, grabbed me for a big hug and then kissed me hard on the mouth.

Chapter Ten

Much to my surprise, she had stashed a small nylon pup tent in the storage compartment of her kayak. We pulled the kayaks up to where they were high and dry. Then we set up the tent on the sand farther up the shore, swatting mosquitoes the whole time. When she invited me inside, she was giggling.

We had no sleeping bags, but we had each other. Neither of us spoke a word as we lay down in our damp clothes on the floor of the tent. I was a little shy at first, I have to admit, but then I reached out, put my arms around her and pulled her to me. She laid her head on my shoulder, and we fell asleep like that.

In the morning, we peeked out from the door of the tent. The sky was blue and brilliant. Seagulls circled around the cove, and around us on the shore tiny sparrows were singing. The spruce trees around us looked full of life as well. It was like we had arrived at our own personal Garden of Eden.

"They'll know we slipped off last night by now," I said.

She nodded and then produced a crushed box of corn flakes from the pack she had stashed in her kayak. She ate a handful and passed it to me. "Sorry, this is all the food I could steal."

I reached into the box and ate a handful of the slightly soggy cereal. "Do you think Chris and the others will come looking for us?"

She shook her head. "They may make a quick search nearby, but after that, I think they'll call the police and maybe the Coast Guard."

"Holy crap," I said.

"You scared?"

"I'm cool," I said. "You?"

"Yeah, a little. But we've made the move now. All we have to do is see it through. Any second thoughts on this?"

"No. I love it out here. And I love being with you."

She smiled then, and that made me think I'd made the right decision. Everything was going to be just fine.

I was still chewing my second mouthful of cornflakes when she said, "Let's get going."

We knocked the tent down, tied it up and stashed it in her kayak. I handed Brianna her life jacket and hitched it up on her. I put mine on. Within minutes, we were back in the water. Brianna studied the compass mounted on the deck of her boat. East again. This time out across a broad open stretch of water.

There was a light sea breeze and more gulls. In open water, I felt the boat was less steady. I could see Brianna also having some trouble keeping her balance. I reminded her we needed to head directly into the waves more to keep from getting dumped. "Wrong direction," she said.

But I had learned a few things back at camp. "It's called tacking, remember? We might need to go a bit upwind first

and then turn and go downwind."
I paddled harder and got ahead of her
and made sure she followed my lead.
She did.

It took us about three hours to cross
the open water and finally come in close
to yet another rocky island. I insisted
we go around it on the side facing the
mainland, the lee side.

"Why?" she asked, sounding annoyed.

"We'll be more protected from the
wind and waves. Easier paddling."

She knew I was right, and she smiled.
"Always looking for the easy way," she
said. But I knew she was joking.

That's when I heard the helicopter
engine. I pointed to a speck in the sky
in the distance. "It's headed this way.
Could be looking for us."

I led us in near the island's shoreline, and we went into a small bay
with high rocks. There was no place to

beach the kayaks and hide them. But there was a place where the rocks jutted out over the water. Not exactly a cave, but a place we could hide. "In there," I said. Brianna followed.

We pulled in as tight to the rock wall as we could, and I lay my paddle down over her boat and mine. "Do the same," I said.

She did. We were now steadied by having temporarily linked our two hulls together. Chris had taught me this trick. It wasn't easy with the sea moving up and down, but we stayed like that for fifteen minutes as we heard the helicopter come in low nearly right over us. It was red and white, and I was pretty sure whoever was in it was looking for something. Looking for us.

"Coast Guard," I said. "They're searching for us." But there was no way they would have seen us.

We lifted paddles and got ready to continue on. "You are so good at this," Brianna said.

I felt a little adrenaline buzz as I took several deep strokes and pulled away from the island into the deeper water. I felt good about being in the water, and about what I had learned about the sea and about kayaking. I was good at this. Good at escaping, maybe. Good at making sure Brianna got safely away. And as we paddled on to the next smaller island, I realized that it was me in the lead now, with Brianna following behind. I was going to make sure we got safely to where we needed to go.

Chapter Eleven

It was getting windier through the day, but we island-hopped, tucking in behind as many of the small islands as we could to stay protected from wind and waves. We saw a few fishing boats in the distance, and the helicopter came back over us once on its return to wherever it had come from. But we found another little cove, and this time we were hidden in the woods.

As we lay there on the forest floor resting, Brianna said the strangest thing. "This is better than dealing drugs," she said.

I gave her a funny look.

"No. I mean, like, this is something real. Selling weed had a certain thrill to it. I knew I was breaking the law, but I didn't feel like I was doing anything wrong. I liked the danger. I liked living by my own rules. But this is better. This is like really taking charge of my own life."

It might sound crazy, but I felt exactly the same way. And I knew she wouldn't have made it this far without me. That made me feel important— responsible. I couldn't say that out loud to her. Instead, I gave her a hug.

We were both starving by then, and I insisted we stop for the day, save our strength and figure out how we were going to eat.

"You set up the tent, and I'll try to find some food," I said.

"Sure."

I had listened a bit during those wilderness survival sessions. Funny thing. I'm sure Chris had no idea he was preparing me for our escape. But I was a good student. I found blueberries. Lots of blueberries that I collected in a plastic bag. A few blackberries as well, but they were pretty sour and I didn't think we should eat too many.

Down by the shoreline, I dug down where I saw air holes and found clams. In the water, there were mussels clinging to rocks, and really large snails among the seaweed. I returned to camp with as much as I could carry.

Brianna dove right into the blueberries. "But I don't think I can eat any of that other stuff," she said.

"It's all good. Even the snails. Escargot, right? Like the French eat."

"Raw?"

"Hmm." Even I wasn't sure I could eat any of it raw. "You have matches, right?"

"Yep. In that waterproof container I stole from camp."

"We start a fire."

"Not sure that's a good idea," she countered.

"I know, but here's what we do. We'll make a small fire, cook these and then put the fire out within a half hour." I found a large flat outcropping of rock. I set the sea creatures on it and covered them with sand. I placed dry spruce needles and tiny twigs on top and lit them with my first match. I piled on dry sticks and quickly had a good blaze. There was very little smoke. I knew we had to eat, and I was pretty sure we could get away with not being spotted. We munched on the blueberries as we waited.

When the fire was out, I used a stick to poke around in the sand and fish out our food. I rinsed everything with seawater and ate the first mussel. It tasted great. I held out one for Brianna.

"I always hated seafood," she said.

"But you'll love this," I told her and dropped a cooked mussel into her mouth.

After that we ate it all—the clams were great, the mussels awesome and the snails were just, well, a little weird, but we ate them anyway. I should have thought ahead and cooked more to save for later, but I didn't.

That night we talked for hours and fell asleep in each other's arms.

I awoke in the middle of the night thinking about my parents. I suddenly felt guilty. I'd caused a lot of trouble for them before, but nothing quite like this. I'd call them, I told myself. But not until we were long gone. Montreal. Brianna and me far from here, living a life together in Montreal. It would be great.

But first we had to get there.

The next day was really windy but quite warm. The plan was to get some more distance covered. Brianna figured we were halfway to Port Joseph.

The first hour of paddling was not so bad, but the wind kept increasing. We had to paddle almost directly into the wind to stay stable, and we were getting very wet and not making much headway.

"We need to head to the mainland," I said finally, shouting so she could hear. I wanted to tell her what I feared most. That the tropical storm, possibly a hurricane, was coming in as predicted, but I didn't get that far. I watched a wave, larger than the rest, break over the bow of Brianna's kayak. She took the full wet smack of it in the face, and I yelled out her name.

But as I was focused on her, I hadn't realized I had turned my kayak sideways to the next incoming waves. The next larger wave broke right on top of me, and I rolled to the side. In a second, I was down in the cold water, still locked into my kayak. Chris would not be there to pull me out this time. Damn. I felt myself being dragged with the boat, but I was underwater and had no control. And I couldn't breathe.

I was pretty sure I was going to drown. I was struggling and panicking.

But then a funny thing happened. I suddenly knew what I had to do. I slowly pushed my body downward from the kayak—down and free of the boat. I released my legs from the cockpit and then swam to the surface, where I heard

Brianna screaming my name. She was trying to come toward me but kept getting hit by wave after wave.

Gasping for breath, I tried to figure out what to do.

The waves seemed to be getting bigger. The water was really rough. We were far from the mainland. My boat was upside down. If Brianna got wasted now, we'd both be in big trouble. She steadied herself and fought hard to make her way to me. She seemed to understand that she had to keep her boat facing straight into the waves to keep from getting dumped.

All of a sudden, I knew that we were in a much more dangerous situation than I had ever imagined. And it was my fault. I had taken charge and got us into this. I was so angry at myself, but knew I had to stay cool. I was gasping for breath, but I said, "It's okay, Brianna. I know what to do."

I didn't really know what to do. But I had to do something. The waves kept bashing us relentlessly.

I grabbed hold of my paddle floating nearby and then hoisted myself over the upturned kayak and tugged it over until it was upright. But it was completely filled with water. It had floatation chambers in the front and back. It wouldn't sink, but it was still one heavy, flooded boat. Damn.

On a calm day, I could have got myself into it, even full of water, and begun bailing with the small bucket and pumping with the emergency pump lashed inside for that purpose. But this was different.

I thought about the predicament we were in. I thought about me. But then I thought about Brianna. If we stayed here much longer, if she tried to help me, she was sure to swamp as well.

I held on to my paddle—I'm not sure why. But I held it with one arm, said goodbye to my swamped kayak and swam, one-armed, toward Brianna, who had just taken another wave full in the face.

When I reached her, I grabbed on to the top strapping that kept the storage hatch sealed and said, "You have to turn us around and head away from the wind."

She looked puzzled and scared. I was out of breath and having a hard time talking. I had swallowed a lot of water. "Now!" I screamed at her. I knew that if we didn't do this immediately, we'd both be in big trouble.

She started to make the turn, and I used my body weight to help keep us balanced.

We barely made it fully around before the next wave slammed down on us from the rear. She got soaked again, but her spray skirt was still in place so we didn't take on water. Looking behind us, however, I realized my abandoned kayak was about to smash down on top of us with the very next wave.

It took all my strength to pull myself up onto the top of her kayak. But it was all I could think of doing. Brianna bravely kept us steady as I did this, and finally I was sitting astride the kayak behind Brianna, feeling a bit high and unsteady. But at least I was above water. And I hung on to my paddle, despite the fact that the sea had tried its best to steal it from me.

We didn't speak after that. We both paddled like mad as the next wave reared up and we saw the other kayak about to be driven into us.

I leaned back as we began to move suddenly faster—caught now by the incoming wave and riding down the front slope of it.

We nearly lost it as the bow of the kayak reached the bottom of the wave and began to plunge into the water, but I leaned back farther.

After that one passed, I realized that maybe we had a chance. I kept my legs locked tight around the hull. Brianna and I paddled as hard as we could.

The wind kept increasing, and the waves became more persistent. When they broke, they broke over us and from behind. We got hammered over and over. But we didn't swamp. All we needed to do was keep moving steadily away from the wind with the waves behind us.

There was another island ahead. And as the waves propelled us, we moved faster. Neither of us said a word. We were paddling for our lives.

Chapter Twelve

Brianna didn't speak as we struggled to keep ourselves moving and steady. As we approached the island, I could see that there was no easy way to put us ashore. There were high jagged rocks all along the front, and we both knew we'd be smashed if we tried to get anywhere close to them.

"We need to go around to the back of the island," I shouted.

"My arms…I can barely move them. I don't know if I can."

I felt much the same way. This wasn't like anything we'd done before. This was a constant struggle. "I don't think we have a choice," I told her.

"We're not going to make it," she said.

It was the first time I'd heard her say anything like this. I knew she was really scared. So was I. I used all my strength to change our course slightly so we would not be going straight to the island but off to one side. The island wasn't very big. If we could get around it, we'd be somewhat sheltered from the wind and waves. We'd have a chance.

Just then we got slammed by a wave that was bigger than all the rest. I felt it coming and braced myself. Brianna screamed when the water came down on top of us. I held tight to my paddle and used it to brace us and keep us balanced.

The wave had pushed us rapidly forward, and I could see we were getting too close to the rock face of the island. I dug in my paddle after the wave had passed and turned us to the right. I knew Brianna was dead tired, but she kept paddling.

We were being drawn by the waves and currents straight toward the jagged rocks as we both struggled to move us away. There was a break in the incoming waves, and I knew it was our only chance. "Paddle harder!" I shouted.

She nodded, and I knew she understood. Now or never.

After several desperate minutes, we slid past the final outcropping and were caught by a strong landward current that pulled us along the side of the island. And I realized we were getting to where we needed to be. The waves were still coming from behind us now, but they were pushing us faster and not breaking.

I think it was more luck than skill.

The wind continued to get stronger and stronger, but that too was in our favor. Finally we were able to begin to turn into the calmer waters behind the island, and I saw a sandy stretch up ahead. Brianna knew we were out of the worst of it and stopped paddling. I think her arms just gave out. So I did what needed to be done. And then, at last, we were finally sliding up onto the gravelly beach with a grinding sound that was the most beautiful thing that I'd ever heard.

I just fell over onto the sand as Brianna pulled the release on the spray skirt and struggled free. She fell down beside me and hugged me with all her might.

We lay there, breathing heavily when suddenly the skies opened up and a heavy rain began to pour down on us. "It's the hurricane," I said, still rather breathless. My words almost got lost, the sound of the rain and wind was so powerful. I knew we were still in plenty of trouble.

Brianna clung to me. "It's like we're being punished."

But I knew it wasn't that. It was bad timing, bad luck and not taking things seriously enough. We'd been reckless. I thought we'd been brave. But it wasn't that.

The rain continued to pound down on us, and I knew we couldn't just lie there. Brianna had her fingernails digging into my side. Her eyes were closed. Neither one of us felt like we had any energy to move. But we had to. I loosened her grip, stood up and felt dizzy, wobbly. I could barely stay standing.

But I grabbed the rope on the front of the kayak and dragged it up the beach as high as I could go. Then I went back for Brianna, lifted her to her feet, and we trudged up the steep incline of the beach as the rain suddenly stopped.

"Thank god, that's over," she said.

"It's not over. It's just beginning. If this is the hurricane they predicted coming ashore here, we need to get to someplace safe. That was just a little rainstorm. The real thing will come later. I think we're going to have to find some way to get help."

"No," she said emphatically, pushing me away suddenly. "I'm not going back there. I know where they'll send me now, and I know it's not going to be some summer camp."

She didn't need to worry. We were on an uninhabited island. The weather was going to be god-awful. If they had been looking for us, they would give up the search when the real storm hit.

We were on our own.

Chapter Thirteen

Despite the sudden change to good weather, I felt in my bones that things would only get worse. I pulled the kayak even farther up into the forest and lashed it to a sturdy spruce tree. I tied the two paddles as well and opened the sea hatch, hauled out the tent and the few supplies. Brianna didn't look too happy.

"Cameron, I think I'm going to have to continue on without you," she said.

"You can't do that," I said.

"Don't worry. When I get ashore, I'll have someone phone and tell them about you. Someone will come and get you."

"It's not that," I insisted. "It's you. You can't go back out there."

It was still windy but very warm, and the sun was out.

"I got you ashore, didn't I? I can handle this," she said. "I'll go toward the mainland and hug the shoreline. I got this far, didn't I?"

I was getting mad at her now. "You can't go back out there," I shouted.

"I don't like people telling me what to do," she snapped back. "And I don't like being shouted at."

I calmed myself. "If you go back out there now, I think you might die."

"Nobody would even care," she said, now sounding more hurt than angry.

"You got that wrong," I said. "You need to stay here with me tonight. We have to ride this storm out. Tomorrow we'll come up with a plan." I didn't know what else to do to make her see my point, so I kissed her hard on the mouth. She pulled away a little at first but then suddenly changed, and she kissed me back.

In about an hour, the wind came up stronger, and the sky began to get darker. We wandered into the forest. I knew the tent wasn't going to be enough to keep us dry and safe. Halfway up a small rocky hill, there was a stone outcropping facing away from the wind. We stopped. We were both exhausted.

"Here," I said. "This is the best we're going to find. We'll tuck in there and wrap ourselves in the tent. "It's gonna be one hell of a night."

She smiled at me—almost a shy smile. The girl was tough, but she had no idea what we were in for. I had been outside once at Lawrencetown Beach when a hurricane had come ashore. You could lean into the wind, and it would hold you up. It was wild. Stuff was flying through the air, and I got hit in the head with a piece of asphalt shingle that gave me a large cut. They said that it was a Category 2. What Chris had said was that this one might be a Category 3. That could be deadly.

There was a flat area covered with moss under the rock outcropping. It wasn't exactly a cave, but it was the best shelter we were going to find. I rooted in the pack and found the water-proof container with five matches left.

"I'm gonna make a fire," I said. "Get us dry and dry out the tent. And then we're going to stay put right here until it's all over."

She nodded. I began to gather dry twigs and pine needles from beneath the rock and bigger branches from nearby. Without saying another word, Brianna began to gather more dead wood. It took two of the precious matches, but I got a fire going. All the damp wood made for too much smoke, but soon I had a big blaze with flames leaping when the wind gusted. I wanted to go back to the shoreline to search for clams and mussels, but I was afraid to leave her. We kept the fire going for two hours until we were mostly dry.

It was late afternoon, and the wind was getting stronger. We sat on the life jackets and wrapped up in the tent beneath the rocky outcropping. I meant to just close my eyes for a minute and rest, but I fell asleep. So did Brianna, I guess.

I awoke later in the pitch-dark to the howling, horrifying sound of wind. Not far away, I heard a tree snap in half and topple to the ground. The fire was out, and rain was driving down in buckets. We were protected from the worst of it, but the sound was as frightening as anything I had ever heard. Brianna was awake as well. She was clinging to me, and I held tightly to her. She was speaking to me, but her words were lost in the sound of the storm around us. Trees were being uprooted and knocked to the ground. Branches were breaking off and flying through the air. We could not see a thing, but the sound was terrifying.

We clung to each other for hours in the deafening roar. Alone on an island like this in the middle of a hurricane, I knew that our survival depended upon keeping our wits, staying put and doing nothing but wait it out.

And then the wind began to diminish. I had never experienced anything like that in my life. We remained tightly wrapped in our tent like a cocoon. I had chosen well. The rocks had protected us. Eventually Brianna, still clinging to me, fell asleep. My plan was to try and stay awake until I was sure the storm was completely over but exhaustion overtook me and I fell asleep as well.

In the morning when I awoke, I was alone. Brianna was nowhere in sight, and what had once been a forest on the hillside now looked like a war zone.

Chapter Fourteen

I knew that Brianna was one crazy girl, but I wasn't ready for this. I called out her name over and over as I began to stumble through the maze of fallen trees. I was hoping I was wrong, but I had no choice but to head for the shoreline. Nothing of the island looked like anything we had seen the day before. There were few standing trees left, and I had to climb over piles of fallen limbs and trees to make headway to get to the water.

When I got there, the kayak was gone. My paddle was still there, and she had left me the backpack with the matches inside. There was a note on a scrap of paper inside the pack.

Dear Cameron,
I'm sorry. I really am. You are the best thing that ever happened to me. I think I love you. I will send help, I promise, but you will never see me again.
Love,
Brianna

The sky was blue now. The sea looked brown and frothy, and there were still large waves rolling by, but the wind was just a light breeze now. If I looked up and away across the water, it was as if nothing at all had just happened.

I sat down on a smooth wet rock, feeling more alone and sad than I had ever felt in my life.

She was out there somewhere, still headed toward Port Joseph, still planning to escape and run to Montreal. And she'd left me behind.

Brianna was in real danger though. The waves would be treacherous out beyond the protection of shore. And she was alone. She was tough, but not that tough.

I sat frozen for nearly twenty minutes. It was like I was paralyzed—my mind and my body. I wanted to shake myself and make this all go away. But I had to face the reality of what I'd let us get into. What I felt now was much worse than the fear I had felt during the hurricane.

Finally, I got up. I looked around. I decided to walk the shoreline of the island. Maybe she tried to leave and was washed back in, or maybe I could see her if I looked in all directions. It seemed pretty hopeless, but it was the only thing I could do. I put on the backpack and picked up my paddle and began to pick my way along the rocky shoreline, heading east toward the seaward-facing part of the island. There was washed-up debris and fallen trees to climb over. It was slow going.

When I first saw it, I thought it was some kind of trick my eyes were playing on me. It was just a flash of orange in a mass of seaweed up along the tree line. I stopped and looked at it in disbelief.

My kayak had washed ashore in the storm. As I stumbled toward it, wobbling on the boulders, I knew that it was probably smashed, but it was buried in kelp and rockweed, and I couldn't really tell. I knelt down and slowly began to pull the seaweed off.

It was damaged, yes, and filled with water and more seaweed. But as I unearthed it, I began to pray that it would be seaworthy. I had not prayed in a long time. But I prayed.

Some cracks in the hull, but no real holes. The rudder was smashed, but I knew I could still steer with my paddle if I had to. I took a hard look at the sea in front of me. The waves were large, and I knew how difficult they could be. Was I really getting ready to go out there?

I decided to shut my mind down, to stop thinking about anything but bailing water out of the kayak. I ran along the shoreline until I found a cracked plastic pail that had washed in. I began to furiously bail the seawater from the boat and couldn't believe how much was in there. My heart was pounding. I knew that for each minute that went by, Brianna would be farther and farther away. If she was still afloat.

Finally, I had emptied enough water so that I could flip the boat over and drain the rest. Funny, I kept thinking that something—I don't know what—would happen and I wouldn't really have to face up to the sea journey. But here it was.

I had worn my life jacket through the night. I had a paddle. And I now had a boat to follow Brianna. I dragged the kayak along the shoreline looking for an easy place to launch where the waves were not slapping hard on the shoreline. Looking east, I saw the next island. For the most part, Brianna and I had been island hopping, staying on the landward side to avoid the larger waves and the wind. As I slid the kayak into the water, I almost chickened out. I had no spray skirt. It wouldn't take much to swamp me. I took the pail because I knew I'd have to bail water slopping in. All I had to do was keep the little boat upright and keep me inside. Keep the waves behind me. Keep my brain focused. Damn. How had I got myself into this?

I sat in the kayak in the shallows and took a long, deep breath. This was a very bad idea. I now blamed Brianna for getting us into this mess. I suddenly wasn't sure she was worth dying for. I put my hands on the side of the boat and began to lift myself out. No way was this going to work.

And then something stopped me. I was halfway out of the boat when this voice in my head told me that if I didn't go after her, I'd regret it for the rest of my life. I dropped back down into the seat. An image of Brianna smiling appeared in my head.

Maybe I would drown out there. But at least I would die trying to save her. I tightened the straps on the life jacket, jammed my paddle into the sand and slid off into the waves.

Chapter Fifteen

The sea was not choppy, but the waves were powerful enough to swamp me at any minute. I spent as much effort keeping upright as I did trying to paddle forward. I had never felt so alone in my life. My mind was racing. What would I do if I found her drowned? What would I do if I found her alive and we got out of this okay? What would I do differently in my life?

My brain went to any number of crazy places, but my arms kept working. As I neared the next island, I had settled into this thought: I am out here on my own, and I am at the mercy of much larger forces. That hurricane was more powerful and violent than anything I had ever experienced. My night with Brianna was as frightening, yet as amazing, as anything I'd ever known. And now I was here, at sea, following her. Trying to save her. Trying to save me.

My arms ached, and my body told me to give up. Go ashore at the next island. Yet, as I rounded the back of the island and the protected waters suddenly became calmer, I regained my strength and my resolve. I did not go ashore. Instead, I focused on the next, much smaller, island farther east. I rounded a sandy spit of land and charged out into the open waters again. There were hundreds of tiny islands out here, but I wanted to believe I could instinctively know where Brianna would go next.

I forced myself to go ashore at the next island and stretch my legs, which were badly cramped. I ate a few blueberries that were growing there and stuffed more in my pockets. I found a tiny pool of fresh water left from the rains and drank deeply, wishing I had a container to carry some of it with me.

Then I pushed off again, my dedication to finding Brianna stronger than ever. I fought off the demons of fear and doubt in my head and focused on the next, much larger, island in the distance. When I got slapped by two waves larger than the rest, I got drenched but kept the little boat steady, turning away from the waves until the swells had passed by.

I bailed with my plastic bucket as best I could and, laden with water that would slow me more, kept the island in my sights and worked the paddle as if my energy was limitless.

The bright sunlight sparkling on the water made me squint, and my vision seemed to blur, but as I neared the island, I saw something—something red. I paddled even harder.

It was a kayak, for sure. Brianna's. As it came into focus, I could see that it was floating near shore, upside down. I felt a cold wave of panic sweep through my head. I told myself to stop thinking. Just paddle. And I thought about those larger forces again. Not just the sea, the storm. But something was guiding me. I'd never been a religious person, and I can't say I had a name for what the force was. But it was inside of me, yet something much larger than just me. Whatever it was, it drove the panic away, it made me feel stronger and it urged me on.

I pulled ashore alongside of Brianna's red kayak. She was nowhere in sight. I pulled her kayak up onto the beach and flipped it over. There was no spray skirt. No paddle. She had dumped it at sea. I scanned the water, hoping not to see what I feared most.

I was about to head back out to search for her, not knowing if this just happened or if she'd swamped hours ago. It was as if time had ground to a halt.

But then she appeared, walking along the shore toward me. I began to run to her, but my legs were cramped from being seated in the kayak for so long. I guess I looked pretty funny—limping along. Just as I was about to reach her, I tripped on a beach stone and fell right into her. We tumbled to the sand beneath us, and I couldn't speak.

As we lay there, all she said was, "Hold me, Cameron. Just hold me and never let me go."

Chapter Sixteen

We stayed on the island for two days. The weather was good and much warmer than usual for the Nova Scotia coast. We swam in the tidal pools in crystal-clear seawater. We found enough fresh water, and mussels and clams to eat, although we had to eat them raw. The matches were gone.

"Let's never leave," Brianna said. "They'll stop looking for us, and we can just stay here forever."

"I'd like that," I said. But I knew it was a complete fantasy. While Brianna was sleeping in the morning, I had fashioned a usable kayak paddle from a piece of driftwood. I had cleaned up both kayaks, and they were ready to go.

On the third day, the sea was completely calm and the sun was bright. We were both feeling a little sick from eating nothing but the shellfish. I was worried one of us might get really ill.

"Today's the day," I said. "We need to go ashore."

Brianna looked at me sadly. "What about forever?"

"I'll stay with you," I said. "I'll go with you to Montreal like we planned. We'll meet your cousin. We could be there in a few days." I was about to tell her a story—repeating her story about the two of us and the new life we would start in Montreal, but she cut me off.

"There is no cousin," she said bluntly. "I made that up."

I was a little shocked and confused. Why had she lied to me? "We'll find another way. We can do it."

But she shook her head. "I've tried before. Something always happens. I get sent back." I had not seen this side of Brianna before. She had always been so feisty, so confident in herself, so strong. Now she seemed like a weak, hurt little girl. I held her in my arms again, but even though we were still together, alone on our island, I felt her slipping away.

We sat in silence for a long time, just staring at the water and at the shore of the mainland to the north. And then I took her to the kayaks and showed her my makeshift paddle. She put on her life jacket, and I handed her the good paddle.

We dragged the kayaks from the bushes and settled them into the water. I helped her in and gave a little push. "I'm okay now," she said. "Whatever happens, we'll always have this."

It was a slow trip across the water to the mainland. We were in no hurry. I tried to talk to her about what we could do once we got ashore—where we could go and how we could still make a life together.

"I'm tired of running away," she finally said.

I wanted to find the right words to make her believe and to make me believe that it would all turn out all right. But I couldn't do it.

We came ashore near a gravel road at the tip of a headland. There was a single shack there, the home of an old fisherman who introduced himself as Jack Kaiser. He had been watching us approach through his binoculars and was there to greet us when we arrived.

"Hell of a storm," he said by way of greeting. Even here on the mainland, hundreds of trees had been knocked down by the hurricane. "You lived through it out there?"

I nodded. I told him who we were. I told him the whole story.

"You are two of the luckiest people I ever met," was his response.

Brianna smiled at me then, and I felt love and longing and loss at the same time. Nothing would ever be the same again in my life.

"I got a truck, if you want me to take you somewhere. I'm not going to turn you in or anything. That's not my style."

I knew he was telling the truth.

We went inside Jack's home, and he fed us and told us some stories about his life and how his wife had died and left him there to live alone.

Later in the day, Brianna shocked me by asking Jack to drive us back to the camp. I tried talking her out of it, but she insisted.

Chris looked as if he was seeing a pair of ghosts when we arrived. He gave me a hug, and he held on to Brianna's hand. "We'd given up hope."

Everybody else had left before the hurricane came ashore, and Chris was the only one left to close down the place for the season. There were no harsh words, and he even let Brianna and me spend the night together. "Just don't tell anyone I let you do this," he said. We promised we wouldn't.

In the morning, Chris drove us to the city. "You're both going to have to do some correctional time. I was hoping the camp thing would change all that, but your adventure made for some serious attention. But first I'm going to take you both to your homes. We'll be back in touch tomorrow to talk about what happens next. Just don't screw it up. You need to work with the system."

I'd heard those words before and always despised them. I knew we'd be sent to separate facilities, and I knew there would be a good chance Brianna, despite what she said, would run away again.

When she got out of the car at her house, she just looked at me, and I couldn't read her look. There was so much more I wanted to say to her, but before I could, her parents had run out the door and were hugging her. Chris said a few words to them, and then we were driving off.

He knew what I was feeling, but he didn't quite know what to say.

Then he finally turned his head a bit and said, "You'll get over her."

But I knew he was dead wrong about that.

Lesley Choyce spends time on the waters of the Eastern Shore of Nova Scotia when not writing for teens and running his own publishing company. His latest books for Orca include *Reckless* and *Reaction*.